HANS CHRISTIAN ANDERSEN

THE STEADFAST TIN SOLDIER

CYNTHIA RYLANT · JEN CORACE

ABRAMS BOOKS FOR YOUNG READERS
NEW YORK

The art in this book was made with watercolor, gouache, arcylic and pen and ink on Arches watercolor paper.

Cataloging-in-Publication Data has been applied for and may be obtained from the Library of Congress.

ISBN: 978-1-4197-0432-1

Text copyright © 2013 Cynthia Rylant
Illustrations copyright © 2013 Jen Corace
Book design by Chad W. Beckerman

Published in 2013 by Abrams Books for Young Readers, an imprint of ABRAMS. All rights reserved. No portion of this book may be reproduced, stored in a retrieval system, or transmitted in any form or by any means, mechanical, electronic, photocopying, recording, or otherwise, without written permission from the publisher.

Printed and bound in China
10 9 8 7 6 5 4 3 2 1

Abrams Books for Young Readers are available at special discounts when purchased in quantity for premiums and promotions as well as

For JDM . . . That's how it is. That's how it goes. —J.C.

fundraising or educational use. Special editions can also be created to specification. For details, contact specialsales@abramsbooks.com or the address below.

115 West 18th Street
New York, NY 10011
www.abramsbooks.com

THERE ARE SOME WHO BELIEVE TOYS

cannot love, but this is far from true. Toys have their own mysterious lives and adventures that we may never know, and love can certainly play its part.

For a steadfast tin soldier, love was indeed everything.

He lived in a Box of Twenty-Five, and he was the twenty-fifth. His twenty-four brothers were as fine as he, being made of tin that made them strong and dressed handsomely in uniforms of blue and red. They were quite the regiment.

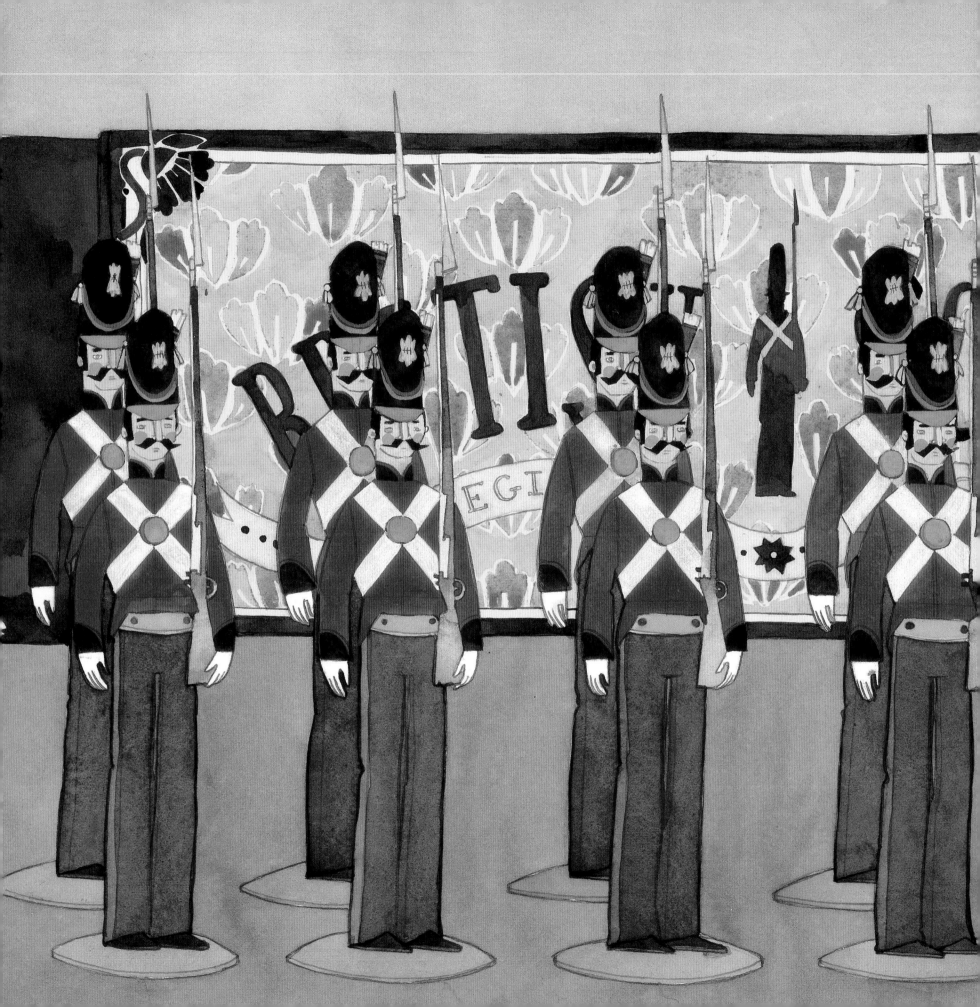

The steadfast tin soldier was as upright and brave as all the rest, but he was also different. For while his brothers had all been made with two perfectly good legs, the steadfast tin soldier had been made with just one. Such things happen and are generally no one's fault. This did not prevent the tin soldier from being as brave as all the others. In fact, it perhaps made him braver.

In the toy room where he lived day after day there was a beautiful dollhouse, and since its inhabitants preferred to stay inside, the steadfast tin soldier hardly ever gave it a glance.

Then one day the little dancer appeared. She stood by the dollhouse door as though to welcome one and all, and she wore a ballerina dress of the finest netting, her cheeks like roses, her eyes blue and bright, and most amazingly of all, she balanced on one leg! Just as the steadfast tin soldier!

Lined up with his brothers who simply stared at the wall, the tin soldier stared at her. And she stared back, smiling, balancing so delicately on her ballerina toes.

They knew they were meant for each other.

Now, when two who are meant to be together first find one another, life almost always throws a stone over which they must stumble.

The stone in this case was a goblin.

The goblin lived in a matchbox that was not nearly as colorful as the soldier's grand container or the comforting dollhouse across the room. No, the matchbox was quite shabby, and perhaps this is what made the goblin so jealous of others' happiness.

He watched the steadfast tin soldier and the little dancer staring at each other day after day. He knew love was in the air. And being a goblin, he hated this.

So one day he pushed the steadfast tin soldier right out the window. The Boy had lined up several toys on the sill, and naturally everyone thought the Boy had just been clumsy and dropped the poor soldier.

But the goblin had pushed him.

Down, down the steadfast tin soldier fell, and when he landed he was quite upside down. It is very hard to be dignified when one has landed upside down. But the soldier managed to be as proud as ever, as all soldiers should in difficult times.

In the toy room,
the little dancer could not
take her eyes off the windowsill,
where the curtain fluttered and the
goblin grinned. The little dancer
would not give the goblin the
satisfaction of seeing her cry. Her
cheeks remained pink, her eyes
stayed blue and bright, and
still she kept her balance,
as all dancers should in
difficult times.

Down below, the steadfast tin
soldier waited to see what would
happen next.

Along came some boys who saw him
and were very delighted, for even though the soldier
was not in the most flattering of positions, he was
still quite a find. It is not often one gets a free
soldier from a Box of Twenty-Five.

The boys made a smart paper sailing ship for the
tin soldier, and they placed him at its bow and set it
to sea in a nearby gutter.

How regal the soldier looked! He had never
wanted to be anything except a soldier, but it was
quite magnificent to have his own boat!

Off he went. He sailed beneath the blue sky for several minutes, then the sky disappeared and at once he was on a dark sea voyage and sailing was not such a pleasure after all.

A giant rat saw him coming, for giant rats see very well in the dark. The rat rocked the steadfast tin soldier's ship, giving him quite a fright.

"Your passport!" hissed the giant rat. "You go no further without a passport."

The poor tin soldier had no idea what a passport was and, of course, had no answer for the rat.

This made the giant rat very angry, and he was just about to tear the ship to shreds when suddenly a great wave of water came rushing in and swept the tin soldier away from the rat, away from the dark, and put him forth once again into the wide world.

"Free!" thought the steadfast tin soldier.

At that very moment, a fish swallowed both him and his sailing ship in one big bite.

Now this was quite a challenge to the tin soldier, for it is almost impossible to look heroic when one has just been swallowed by a big fish.

But the steadfast tin soldier held himself straight, lying in the long, watery stomach, and he met his fate with courage. The soldier was certain he would never see the little dancer again. He simply had to accept it as his sorrowful lot.

However, just as he was adjusting himself to life in a fish, he was blinded by a great streak of light, and he felt himself being lifted up and put on a table. All around him there was great commotion, but he was so dizzy from his adventures that he could not understand what was happening.

The soldier received a soapy bath. The soap so stung his eyes and he wished he could wipe it away, for he was being carried someplace and wanted to see where he was going.

Then, where should he find himself, when his vision and thinking had cleared? Why, he was right back in the room from which he had unwillingly escaped! And there across the way, as bright and beautiful as ever, his true love glowed with happiness at his return.

And was this the end of the tin soldier's adventures? No, there would be one more, for the goblin was not finished with him.

A few days after the soldier's return, a most strange event occurred. A great fire was burning in the stove, and it needed to be continually fed by the bucket of coal beside it.

No one knows just how the steadfast tin soldier landed in that bucket. But when the next great shoveling occurred, he was part of it! Into the fire he went. The soldier was certain now his happy life was over.

But his story was not yet complete.
For a great draft of wind suddenly
blew down the pipe, and the fiery
stove spit him right back out and
across the room to the little dancer!
The tin soldier was so hot from the
fire that the two instantly melted into
each other's arms.

And so they stayed, the steadfast tin soldier
and the little dancer, forevermore.